PUFFIN BOOKS

Harry's Aunt

Harry's Aunt

Sheila Lavelle

Illustrated by
Jo Davies

PUFFIN BOOKS

PUFFIN BOOKS

Published by the Penguin Group
Penguin Books Ltd, 80 Strand, London WC2R 0RL, England
Penguin Putnam Inc., 375 Hudson Street, New York, New York 10014, USA
Penguin Books Australia Ltd, 250 Camberwell Road, Camberwell, Victoria 3124, Australia
Penguin Books Canada Ltd, 10 Alcorn Avenue, Toronto, Ontario, Canada M4V 3B2
Penguin Books India (P) Ltd, 11 Community Centre, Panchsheel Park, New Delhi – 110 017, India
Penguin Books (NZ) Ltd, Cnr Rosedale and Airborne Roads, Albany, Auckland, New Zealand
Penguin Books (South Africa) (Pty) Ltd, 24 Sturdee Avenue, Rosebank 2196, South Africa

Penguin Books Ltd, Registered Offices: 80 Strand, London WC2R 0RL, England

www.penguin.com

First published by Hamish Hamilton Ltd 1985
Published in Puffin Books 1995
13 15 17 19 20 18 16 14 12

Text copyright © Sheila Lavelle, 1985
Illustrations copyright © Jo Davies, 1985
All rights reserved

Printed and bound in China by Leo Paper Products Ltd

0–140–37530–9

When Harry went to stay with his
Aunt Winnie for the holidays he didn't
know she was a witch.

She didn't look like a witch at all.

It wasn't until after supper that Harry found out.

Aunt Winnie put on a black cloak and a pointed hat. She took an old broomstick from the cupboard and went for a ride around the garden in the moonlight.

Harry couldn't believe his eyes.

The next day Aunt Winnie turned into a chimpanzee in the greengrocer's shop. She climbed on to a shelf and threw oranges and bananas at the surprised customers.

The greengrocer went mad with rage.

On the way home Aunt Winnie
turned into an elephant, on the Number
Five bus. It took six men to get her
free.

"Double fare for an elephant," said the
driver. And he made Harry pay an extra
fifty pence.

In the Post Office on Friday
Aunt Winnie turned into a crocodile.
Everybody ran into the street,
screaming and shouting.

"I'm fed up with this," said Harry.

"I can't help it, Harry," said his aunt.
"I've been changing into all sorts of
things for so long I can't stop. We had
better stay at home for a few days."

Harry agreed. He took the dead bats
and toads out of the larder and threw them
in the dustbin.

On Saturday, Aunt Winnie planted Poison-ivy in the flowerbed. Harry mowed the lawn, keeping a watchful eye on his aunt. She might turn herself into a beetle and fall down a crack in the ground.

Then Mr Mills came by with his dog,
Horace.

"Not going to the Dog Show?" he
said, looking over the fence. "Village
Hall. Two o'clock." And he trotted away.

Aunt Winnie looked at Harry.

Harry looked at Aunt Winnie.

"No," said Harry. "We are *not* going to the Dog Show. It's better if we stay at home."

"But I can't stay at home all my life!" wailed Aunt Winnie. "I'll turn into a cabbage!"

"*That* will make a nice change," said Harry to himself.

But Aunt Winnie got her own way.
She put on her yellow hat with the
poppies on it.

Harry kept close to her all the way to
the Village Hall.

He had a funny feeling in his tummy.
It was a bit like going to the dentist . . .
only worse.

The Village Hall was packed. Harry had never seen so many dogs in his life. He had never heard such a din.

At one end of the Hall was the judge's table, covered in silver cups.

"Well I never," said Aunt Winnie. "There's dear old Mrs Moon."

And she disappeared into the crowd.

"Come back!" shouted Harry.

But his aunt was nowhere to be seen.

Harry climbed on to a chair to look over the heads of the crowd.

Suddenly there was trouble. Dogs ran round the Hall barking and howling. Chairs were knocked over. Benches crashed to the floor. Someone screamed.

Harry stood on tiptoe to see what the trouble was.

It was a cat — a small black cat, ears back
and tail bushed out. It dashed from table
to table, along the windowsills, over a
row of cages, spitting and hissing at the
dogs behind it.

"Oh no! Aunt Winnie's done it
again," said Harry.

People were rushing about, trying to
catch their dogs.

The judge's table fell over with a
crash, and the silver cups rolled all over
the floor.

The cat started to climb up the
curtains behind the stage.

Harry saw his chance.

He leapt down from the chair and
pushed through the crowd.

Harry reached up and grabbed the cat by the scruff of the neck, and pushed his way out of the side door.

Harry's sleeve was torn, his trousers were ripped and his face was scratched and dirty.

"That's it, Aunt Winnie," he told the cat. "I'm never going anywhere with you ever again."

And he ran all the way back to his aunt's cottage, with the cat tucked into his jacket.

Harry dumped the cat on the rug in
front of the fire. He sat in the rocking
chair to wait for his aunt to turn back into
herself again.

Nothing happened.

The cat dozed off in the warmth of
the fire.

Harry prodded the cat with his toe.

"Come on, Aunt Winnie," he said
crossly. "You can't stay like that for ever.
It's nearly teatime."

Just when he was getting really worried, Harry heard a bang at the door. He opened it, and his eyes grew round as dinner-plates.

On the doorstep stood a large black and white dog. In its teeth was a silver cup.

Harry stared.

Then a most extraordinary thing happened.

The dog's back legs and tail disappeared. In their place were Aunt Winnie's wellies and her old green skirt.

Then the dog's front legs and furry
body disappeared. There was Aunt
Winnie's orange cardigan.

Last of all the big black and white head
disappeared. And there was Aunt Winnie's
smiling face, and the yellow hat with the
poppies on it.

"Aunt Winnie!" cried Harry.
"I thought you'd turned into a cat."

"I wouldn't do a silly thing like that,"
said Aunt Winnie. "I turned into an Old
English Sheepdog and won First Prize!"

She put the silver cup proudly on the
shelf above the fireplace.

Harry looked at the cat, still sleeping by the fire.

"What are we going to do with that?" he said.

"Keep it, of course," said Aunt Winnie. "I've always wanted a black cat."

And she took her broomstick from the cupboard and went for a ride over the rooftops before tea.